Rush for Gold

TREASURED HORSES COLLECTION™

titles in Large-Print Editions:

RUSH FOR GOLD

The story of an inquisitive palomino,
a resourceful girl, and their search for treasure

Written by **Coleen Hubbard**
Illustrated by **Sandy Rabinowitz**
Cover Illustration by **Christa Keiffer**
Developed by Nancy Hall, Inc.

Gareth Stevens Publishing
MILWAUKEE

For a free color catalog describing Gareth Stevens' list of high-quality books and
multimedia programs, call 1-800-542-2595 (USA) or 1-800-461-9120 (Canada).
Gareth Stevens Publishing's Fax: (414) 225-0377.

Library of Congress Cataloging-in-Publication Data

Hubbard, Coleen.
Rush for gold / written by Coleen Hubbard;
illustrated by Sandy Rabinowitz; cover illustration by Christa Keiffer.
p. cm.
Originally published: Dyersville, Iowa: Ertl Co., 1998.
(Treasured horses collection)
Summary: In need of two hundred dollars, the entry fee for competing
in the Palomino Parade, Landy hears a local legend about hidden
gold and becomes determined to find the treasure.
ISBN 0-8368-2405-9 (lib. bdg.)
[1. Buried treasure—Fiction. 2. Horsemanship—Fiction.
3. Horses—Fiction.] I. Rabinowitz, Sandy, ill. II. Title.
III. Series: Treasured horses collection.
PZ7.H85668Ru   1999
[Fic]—dc21   99-11707

This edition first published in 1999 by
Gareth Stevens Publishing
1555 North RiverCenter Drive, Suite 201
Milwaukee, Wisconsin 53212 USA

© 1998 by Nancy Hall, Inc.
First published by The ERTL Company, Inc., Dyersville, Iowa.

Treasured Horses Collection is a registered trademark of The ERTL Company, Inc.

Printed in the United States of America

1 2 3 4 5 6 7 8 9 03 02 01 00 99

CONTENTS

Palomino Parade

"**P**lease be there," eleven-year-old Landy Berensen whispered under her breath as she stood in front of the family's large wooden mailbox. The fresh California breeze brushed her face and cooled the heat of the midday summer sun. She glanced anxiously toward her best friend. "Wish me luck," she said.

"Luck," Amie Clark, a freckle-faced brunette with brown eyes, replied.

It was almost a month ago that Landy had written for an entry form to the upcoming palomino horse show. Every day she'd rushed to the mailbox to see if there was a letter addressed to her. So far, every day had ended in disappointment, and she'd trudged back down the gravel road to her house. Today was going to be different, or so she hoped. Amie had received her letter only an hour ago. So maybe, just maybe, Landy's would arrive today, too.

"Here goes," Landy said. She took a deep breath, flipped open the lid to the mailbox, and quickly snatched the clump of mail settled on the bottom. The top envelope was a bill, followed by another.

"The envelope's kind of yellowish," Amie said as she extended her hands to hold the rejects.

Landy fanned the remaining envelopes, flyers, and magazines. "I didn't know we got so much mail."

"There," Amie said, pointing to a business-sized envelope. "That's it."

Landy pinched the corner of the pale yellow envelope and snatched it from the stack. She read the return address written in bold, brown letters: California Buckskin and Palomino Parade, Sacramento, California.

Amie pulled an identical envelope from the back pocket of her blue jeans. "It looks just like mine."

"Did you open yours yet?" Landy asked.

"And break our promise? No way," Amie replied.

Just then a stiff breeze blew through the pine trees, rustling the letters that had tumbled to the ground. "The mail!" Landy cried. She slid her prized envelope inside the pocket of her denim shirt. The girls laughed as they got on their knees to gather the Berensens' mail. With the day's mail in tow, the pair ran down the gravel road leading back to the Berensens' two-acre ranch near Caribou, in northern California.

Caribou was a small town tucked into the Sierras. Landy loved living in the mountains, where she could ride Belle for hours without hearing a car or seeing a stop light. Belle was a strong six-year-old mare. Like most quarter horse palominos, her head was short and wide with a small muzzle. She had long shoulders, powerful hindquarters, and one white sock. Yet Landy knew it was more than Belle's shiny white mane and creamy golden coat that she found attractive. It was the fire and strength that came from within Belle that Landy loved.

Sometimes she and Belle would run through the spring wildflowers, kicking up petals and sweet smells. Other days, she would ride with Amie and Copper, Amie's palomino. Copper was a few shades darker than Belle, but still considered a true palomino. The foursome would go for picnics or run errands in town.

The hours just seemed to fly when she and Belle

were together. And now that summer was here, she had even more time for riding.

Belle was forever leading Landy to brooks and caves that no one ever explored. There was always another field to investigate or hill to climb. Landy loved Belle's curiosity, mostly because it matched her own.

The whole Berensen family liked to ride, and several times throughout the summer they would pack the horses and camp in the mountains. Tomas, Landy's dad, was a forest ranger. He had regions of the national forest to monitor, and sometimes they would make it a family outing. He had also invested a lot in a tree farm, a favorite camping spot for the family.

Landy's mom, Claire, had taught high school for several years, and only recently opened up her own art shop, specializing in pottery. Landy's older brother, Jason, was like most teenage boys. He liked football and girls.

"Mail's here," Landy called to her mom through the screen door. She slapped the stack on the seat of a rocking chair and rushed down the steps to rejoin Amie.

The girls tumbled to the grass and leaned against the white, wood fence that surrounded the pasture.

"Ready," Landy said with a grin. She tucked a strand of long, white-blonde hair behind one ear. "Let's do it."

"You go first," Amie said.

"Together," Landy insisted. "Ready, set, go."

They tore open the bulky envelopes, and Landy began reading aloud. "Welcome to the tenth annual Buckskin and Palomino Parade."

Then Amie began reading. "This show is the largest and most popular in northern California."

"Riders from as far as Spain and India have appeared in the programs," Landy continued. "Imagine riding in a show with someone from Spain!"

"Awesome," Amie said.

"Listen to what it says about the parade class," Landy said as she flipped to page two. "Parade class is set up in three divisions; Maiden, Novice, and Expert."

"What do you think we are?" Amie asked.

"Expert, of course."

Amie raised her eyebrows. "Landy, this is our first big show."

"Okay, maybe we should stick to novice."

Amie shook her head and both girls laughed.

Landy and Amie had ridden in many local horse shows. They were experienced in barrel racing, pole bending, and showmanship. These local contests typically ended with Landy, Amie, and another girl, Monica Tremane, exchanging first-, second-, and third- place awards in their age division.

Although Landy liked the speed and precision of barrel racing and pole bending, and the training of horsemanship, there was something about parading that gave her a feeling of elegance, speed, and accuracy.

"Listen to this," Landy announced, getting back to the letter. "There will be three, one-hour parade class sessions with national and international instructors."

"Horsemanship, presentation, and grooming are only a few of the topics emphasized," Amie added, finding the paragraph where Landy was reading. Amie set the papers in her lap and stared at the sky. "This is so exciting I'm going to burst."

"Hey, there's more," Landy continued. "The top ten riders in each division will compete for the All Around title on the final evening. A trophy and hundred dollar purse will be awarded to the All Around winners."

"This is a dream come true," Amie said.

"And we're going to be there," Landy added. "We'll be so good they'll have to have co–first place winners."

Landy read ahead, devouring every word of the letter. Suddenly, her heart stopped. She turned to the registration sheet and then back to the letter. Had she read something wrong? Were the words in front of her for real? "Whoa," she said. "Have you read the last page yet?"

"Not really." Amie rummaged through the collection of papers. "Why, what's wrong?"

Landy flipped to the last page, pointed to the final paragraph, and read aloud. "To ensure show entry, stable registration, and a spot in the three classes, please send your completed entry form and a check or money order for $200.00."

Peer Pressure

Amie Clark's mouth dropped open. "Two hundred dollars!"

Landy tapped the entry form, "That's what it says."

"Do you have two hundred dollars?" Amie asked.

"In my dreams," Landy said. She couldn't believe that five minutes ago she had been the happiest girl in the mountains.

Amie scratched her head. "I have a college fund started, but I don't think my parents will let me touch it for a horse show."

Landy shook her head and rolled her eyes. "I know mine won't."

"So what are we going to do?" Amie asked.

"I'm not sure yet," Landy said. "This is going to take some serious planning."

"We don't have a lot of time," Amie added. "The show is only a few weeks away."

Landy sat up straight. "Hey, I've got it. If we win the All Around championship, we get a hundred dollars. There's half the registration fee right there."

"Somehow I don't think the officials would go for that arrangement."

Landy nodded in agreement. "It was just a thought."

"We'd better come up with a more practical one."

"Look, our parents said we could go to a horse show this year, right?" Landy said, trying to refuel her excitement.

"I doubt if they thought it would cost this much," Amie answered.

"I'm sure they'll help out."

"I'm sure they will too," Amie added, "but . . ."

Landy interrupted. "Two hundred dollars is a lot of helping."

"Not to mention we don't have even one sequin for a costume yet." Amie's voice started to quiver. "Plus, we'll have to stay in a motel."

"Maybe our first step should be to talk to our

folks and see what we can work out," Landy suggested.

"I guess so," Amie agreed.

"Hey, I've got an idea," Landy said. "We could get a sponsor." She began to get excited again. "Yeah, the grocery store sponsors a baseball team every year. They give them T-shirts and everything. Remember when the high school volleyball team went to the state championships in Los Angeles?"

Amie nodded. "The Country Cobbler and the Book Bin helped out the team."

"There is a problem, though," Amie said.

"What?" Landy asked.

"I refuse to wear a costume with 'Hall's Hardware Store' or 'Grindel & Kelly Fertilizer and Feed Company' plastered all over it."

"You've got a point there," Landy said. "But you've got to admit the idea has possibilities."

"Maybe," Amie conceded.

"Hi, girls." Monica Tremane's voice pierced the air as she rode horseback down the gravel road toward them.

Landy shuddered. If there was anyone she didn't want to talk to now, it was Monica Tremane. Her snooty attitude and continuous bragging grated on her nerves.

"I see you have your applications for the Sacramento show, too, " Monica said, resting comfortably in her saddle.

"Are you going?" Amie asked.

"Well, it's practically required." Monica flipped her leg over the horn and sat in mock side saddle fashion. "I placed second in our age division last year and took third in the All Around. It's like the Miss America pageant. It's my responsibility to crown the new winner, before I move up to first in the All Around."

"Or second," Amie added.

"You might not even place at all," Landy muttered. She kept her eyes down and tugged at the long grass. It took all her powers of restraint not to lash into Monica.

"Last year's show was so thrilling," Monica continued. She ran her fingers through her palomino's mane. "We bought the air-conditioned horse trailer for Achilles. It made a huge difference. Remember, girls, it's very important that your horse is completely comfortable and rested before a show."

Landy sighed. At this rate she'd be lucky if she could ride Belle the 197 miles to Sacramento.

"We stayed at this superb four-star hotel. It's a bit of a drive to the arena, but definitely worth it. And don't get me started on the restaurants," Monica said.

"We won't," Landy muttered.

Amie heard her and bit her lip to hold back a laugh.

"I had crepes, real French crepes, prepared at my table with the freshest ingredients."

"Sounds wonderful," Amie said.

"This year will be even better," Monica rattled on. "I've been practicing with my own private riding coach in San Francisco."

"You've been going to San Francisco for private lessons?" Amie inquired.

"Not just that," Monica continued. "My costumer is there."

Landy had heard enough. "Costumer?"

"Of course," Monica explained. "You don't think I'd rely on the dress shop in Caribou to design my creations."

"What does your costume look like?" Amie asked.

Landy squirmed. She couldn't believe Amie had subjected them to another twenty minutes of boasting. She wished she could walk away, saddle Belle, and go for a long ride into the mountains.

"It's fabulous," Monica said. "Impresario, that's the costume company. They took all my ideas, and together we are developing a character presentation that will knock the boots off the competition."

"So what are you wearing?" Landy asked.

"I'd love to tell you, but I shouldn't reveal any secrets. Let's just say, it's the pièce de résistance."

"Sounds French," Amie said.

"Could be," Monica added, as she tilted her head. "At seventy-five dollars an hour plus materials, it will be stunning."

Monica flipped her leg back to the straddle position. "Well, we'd better be riding along. I just wanted to stop by to see if you'd received your registration materials and were planning to go."

Landy stood up and brushed the pile of torn grass from her lap. "Oh yes, we're going."

Monica picked up the reins, made a clicking sound, and gently tapped Achilles. "One last piece of advice. If you're truly serious about the show, I suggest you be prepared. It's very different from riding at Budman Field or around the mountains. There are ten thousand seats at the Sacramento arena, and all eyes are on you."

"Really?" Amie said.

Monica continued. "Bright lights, strange noises, and hundreds of riders. I've established a quality reputation for myself and Caribou. I'd hate to see it tarnished."

Landy could feel the anger building inside her as Monica rode off. "Tarnish her reputation," she grumbled. "She's made it rusty all by herself." Landy kicked at a clump of dirt on the roadway. "Boy, would I like to knock her down to size."

Amie nudged her shoulder into Landy's. "Relax Landy, she's not worth it."

"I know," Landy said, shaking her head. "Besides, I'll do my knocking in the arena. We'll see who has bragging rights after Sacramento."

"That is if we get to go," Amie replied.

"Oh, we're going all right," Landy said. "As soon as we figure out how to pay for this trip, we'll spend all our time getting ready for this show."

Landy and Amie started walking up the gravel road. "I'll bet Monica was trying to scare us," Landy said.

"Scare us, how?"

Landy stopped walking. "She came over here to find out if we were going to the horse show, right? She blasted us with all that stuff about costumes, air-conditioned horse trailers, and huge crowds to make us think we couldn't do it." Landy stuffed her hands in her pockets and rocked on the heels of her boots. "What she's really worried about is us."

"Us?" Amie asked.

"Of course. She knows that we've beaten her in competitions before. She knows we can do it again."

Amie's eyes lit up. "You may be right."

"Of course I'm right."

Amie shrugged. "It would be nice to have beautiful costumes and a luxury hotel to stay in, though."

"We will," Landy said. "As soon as we solve our money situation, there will be nothing to keep us from winning and having it all, just like we planned."

The girls reached the mailbox. "So, first things first," Landy said. "We'll talk to our parents and find out what we're going to need to do."

"I'll talk to mine right away," Amie stated.

"Call me with the good news!" Landy shouted after her.

Negotiating

Landy grasped the entry form and stepped up on the fence that surrounded the Berensens' pasture, where Belle was grazing.

Temperamentally and physically, Landy and Belle were as alike as a horse and rider could be. They both had hazel eyes and long white-blonde hair that glistened in the sunshine. Their golden skin, Landy's kissed by rays of the California sun and Belle's two shades lighter than a newly minted gold coin, gave them a stunning appearance.

Landy pulled herself up on the fence, swinging her legs over to the pasture side. She rested her boots on the middle board. Belle arrived moments later, to nuzzle affectionately at Landy's ribs.

Belle's official name was Queen Isabella del Conquistador. She was registered with the Palomino Horse Breeders of America, as well as the American Quarter Horse Association. Palomino is a color type rather than a true breed, so Quarter Horses, American Saddlebreds, and Tennessee Walking Horses can all be palominos. Landy didn't care about the fancy papers. She just loved Belle for being Belle.

Landy laughed. "You think there's something in there for you, girl?" She patted Belle's firm neck stroking downward toward her back.

Belle was persistent, prodding for her prize. "What if I forgot them today, pretty girl? What would you do then?" Landy finally held out her palm to reveal a group of small knobby carrots. Belle devoured them in two bites.

"There's something I want to show you," Landy continued. She pulled out the parade entry form. "We're going to a horse show."

The front cover displayed a beautiful palomino standing in a golden field with mountains in the background and a bright blue sky. "That could be you," Landy said, tapping the picture. Belle rubbed her head against the form.

"This is a very important piece of paper," Landy

said. "We're going to ride with a whole bunch of horses and take first place. How does that sound?" Belle tilted her head for an extra scratch.

Landy took a handful of Belle's mane and began braiding it while she talked. "Hey, you don't care about air-conditioned horse trailers do you?" Belle pawed at the ground, and Landy laughed at the response. "I'll take that as a no," she said. "Well, I'm glad because I know I don't care about luxury hotels, swimming pools, and twelve-star restaurants. Sure, it might be nice, but I don't need them, not as long as I have you."

Landy finished the braid and threw her arms around Belle's neck. "Ever since Mom and Dad said I could go out of town to a show, I knew I wanted to go to Sacramento. We're going to have the best time ever." Landy looked toward the house and sighed. "There's just one thing I've got to do first—talk to Mom and Dad about the registration fee." She took the last small carrot from her bag and gave it to Belle. "Wish me luck." She kissed Belle's forehead, swung her legs back, and hopped off the fence.

From the porch, Landy could hear her parents laughing and talking. Landy knew her dad was going on a trip to check fire conditions on the west ridge. He'd be gone for three days, so she needed to talk to them now.

The knot in her stomach turned and twisted. She took a deep breath and opened the screen door that led to the modest living room.

"Mom, Dad," Landy called.

"In here," Claire Berensen called from the kitchen.

Landy pulled off her boots and shuffled in her stocking feet across the hard wood hallway leading into the kitchen.

"Can I talk to you about something?"

"Sounds serious," Claire Berensen answered. She was tall and lean like Landy but had light brown, shoulder length hair that she wore swept up on one side. Mom also loved horses, and Landy was sure she'd understand about the show.

"It's very important," Landy said.

Her mother set a bowl of grapes on the table. "Your father went upstairs to get his backpack."

Landy pulled out her chair at the round table where the family ate their meals. She sat with her hands crossed. "I think I'll wait for Dad."

Her mother nodded before crossing to the bottom of the narrow back staircase that led to the bedrooms upstairs. "Tomas," she called. "Landy would like to talk to us for a minute."

Tomas Berensen emerged from the stairway in his drab green ranger's uniform. He set his bulky pack by the back door and looked at Landy. Landy had inherited her Danish father's towhead white hair, his oval face, and his cheekbones. He pulled out the chair opposite his daughter and sat down. "What's on your mind, kiddo?"

Landy swallowed hard. "Remember when you said I could ride in a horse show outside of Caribou this year?"

"Sure," Mr. Berensen said.

"Well, Amie Clark and I sent away for entry forms to the Palomino Parade in Sacramento."

Her parents exchanged glances.

"I guess you meant *really* out of town," her mother added.

"It's the best parade in the state," Landy blurted. She changed her focus from one parent to the other. "You even said yourself that I'd won just about every contest around here. You said I needed a challenge."

"You did say that," her mother replied, as she winked at her husband.

"You're a very good rider, Landy," her father said. "What are you worried about?"

Landy nervously tapped her fingers on the table. "Like I said, I sent away for the application, and it finally arrived today. The problem is . . ." Landy lowered her eyes and played with the edge of a frayed cloth napkin on the table. "The problem is, I have to send in a two-hundred dollar registration fee."

Her mother sat up straight. "Two hundred dollars for a horse show!"

"That sounds a little steep," her father added. "The ones around here are at the most twenty-five."

"This one has professional parade instructors," Landy responded.

"Two hundred dollars," her mother said again.

"If I win the All Around competition," Landy interrupted, "I'll get a hundred dollars."

Her mother placed her lemonade glass in the sink. "Aren't you counting your chickens before they've hatched?"

"What does the registration fee include?" her father asked.

"It covers three days of classes, stable costs, and riding in the opening ceremonies and in the parade competition," Landy answered.

Her father shrugged. "That doesn't take into account traveling to Sacramento, motels, and food."

"Or costumes or spending money," her mother added.

"But you said I could," Landy begged.

"Let me ask you this." Her father's voice had a familiar tone to it. "How much have you saved so far?"

"Not much," Landy muttered. She wished she

hadn't bought that print top last week when she was in town. "I don't suppose you'd consider letting me borrow some money from my college fund."

"Absolutely not," her mother said firmly.

"I'm willing to do anything to earn money. Clean stalls, work at the tree farm, anything. It could even be part of my Christmas and birthday presents, if that would help."

"Well, those are all possibilities, and maybe by the end of the summer you'll have saved enough," her father stated.

"I can't wait until the end of the summer," Landy cried. "I need the fee in three weeks. Sooner, to ensure a stable. Can't you help me out, and I'll pay you back?"

"It's not only the fee, kiddo. The out-of-town expenses will be pretty steep. You can't go by yourself. Your mother and I can try to arrange our schedules, but you're asking the whole family to fulfill your dream."

"Maybe you need to rethink the Sacramento trip," her mother said. "I'm not saying you can't go out of town, but maybe choose something a little closer, like Chico. We could even make it back the same day if we wanted to. There is always the Fourth of July celebration right here in Caribou, or the Almanor Lake contest you really liked last year. We could make it a family camping and fishing trip as well."

"I don't want to go to Almanor Lake, I want to go to Sacramento." Landy's voice was shaking.

She pushed back her chair and ran out the back door, stumbling down the back stairs in her stocking feet. Salty tears stung her eyes and blurred her vision. She didn't care; she just had to get away. Her feet carried her over the gravel road and down fifty yards to the barn. She flipped up the metal latch to the paddock and wiped her tears on her sleeve. As she closed the gate, she saw Belle walking toward her. Clutching a handful of mane, Landy leapt up on Belle's back, laying her head next to the base of Belle's neck. The tears still flowed, but softened with each step Belle took toward the barn. Landy slid off Belle's back and opened the door to her stall. "I'm sorry, girl," Landy said as Belle walked into her stall. "I won't give up, though," she whispered.

Landy caught her breath, grasped an armful of hay, and placed it in Belle's manger. Still crying, she leaned against the tack room door and slid to the dirt of the barn floor.

With a last sniff, she moved sluggishly into her evening chores. She opened the grain barrels and scooped out Belle's oats and corn, dumping them into the small wooden trough to the left of the hay. She cleaned the water bucket and filled it with fresh water. Taking the brush and curry comb, Landy then groomed Belle. She stopped momentarily to untwist the braid she had so playfully done before she'd talked to her parents. Belle snorted and flexed with the sensation of the comb. Finally, Landy took the brushes back to the tack room and sat with her back against the hay bales.

"Landy," her father called.

"In here," Landy answered, half embarrassed, half dejected.

"I'm sorry, kiddo," her father said.

"Me too," Landy replied.

"I just called the Clarks, and they've been talking to Amie. They said they can drive you girls and the horses."

Landy couldn't believe what she was hearing. Was there still hope? Her heart skipped a beat with excitement.

"This doesn't solve the registration fee problem, but we'll try to work it out. You'll need to show us you can be responsible, though. If you can raise the registration fee, your mother and I will match it to cover the travel expenses."

"Thanks, Dad. Thanks so much!" Landy leapt from her spot on the ground into her Dad's arms. "I won't let you down. I'll show you how responsible I can be."

Picnic Perfect

"Sixty-five dollars and thirty-two cents," Landy said with a sigh. She flopped back onto the pillow of a twin bed in her room. "For a week we've been selling horse rides to tourists, running errands on horseback, cleaning stalls, and we still only have sixty-five dollars and thirty-two cents."

"I'm exhausted," Amie said from her perch on the other twin bed.

Landy stared at the pink and blue flowers stenciled with ivy that wrapped the molding on her ceiling. "Let's take a ride," she suggested.

"How are we going to earn money doing that?" Amie asked.

Landy got off her bed and slipped out of her flowered shorts and into her jeans. "We're not. We're going to clear our heads and start fresh. I don't know about you, but I always get my best ideas when I ride." She grabbed her cowboy hat and jean jacket with the tapestry collar and trim, and the girls headed for the back staircase leading to the kitchen.

After gathering their riding supplies, including bug and sunscreen lotion, picnic food, canteens of water, and canvas bags filled with grain for the horses, they were ready and raring to go.

Landy was thrilled to be on an outing with Belle. It felt like the first time in a week that she hadn't been thinking of ways to earn the registration fee. She patted Belle and took a deep breath of mountain air. The scents of pine and wildflowers filled her head, instead of thoughts of quarters and dimes.

As they turned off the main dirt road and began their ascent into the wilderness, Belle strained with the steep incline. Landy shifted her weight forward trying to match Belle's rhythm and motion. She gently stroked Belle's neck, encouraging her. Within a few minutes they reached the crest and open ground.

"Let's ride over by the grove and have lunch," Amie suggested.

They found a small clearing with a few large

rocks and a gravel shoreline that gently led to a river—a perfect place for the horses to drink. Landy looped Belle's lead rope over a tree branch and proceeded to unpack the lunches.

Landy sat on the top of a flat rock, took off her jean jacket, rolled it up, and placed it behind her head like a pillow. She punched the straw into her juice box and settled in to bask in the sunshine like a lazy lizard in the summer sun.

"What's with Belle?" Amie said.

Landy opened her eyes. Belle was wading into the river. She jumped from her resting place, ran over to Belle, snatched the reins, and pulled her back onto dry land. "Where are you going, girl?" Landy asked.

"Hey, you know Belle," Amie said, "always curious, always looking for something to investigate. Kind of like someone else I know." Amie pointed to her friend and laughed.

Landy grasped the bridle with her left hand and gently stroked Belle's neck. "What do you see, girl?"

Landy squinted into the distance, peering into the mixture of pines and vegetation, then turned back to Amie. "I should have brought the binoculars. Whatever is over there really has got Belle curious."

"I don't even want to know," Amie answered. She was busy gathering a few wildflowers and putting them into her empty canvas bag to take home.

Landy led Belle away from the river and the downwind scent that seemed to have her mesmerized. The girls ate in silence for a moment, but Landy had to admit her curiosity was also piqued. She scanned the opposite shore between bites of her sandwich.

"Don't get any wild ideas," Amie said. "I know that look. You and Belle are the worst at getting into trouble."

"You can stay if you want to," Landy said, "but Belle and I are going to take a closer look."

"I thought we were supposed to be thinking of new money–making projects, not going on a wild goose chase."

Landy snickered. "Who knows, whatever is over there might lead us to a pot of gold."

"I don't see any rainbows," Amie grumbled.

Landy packed up the remainder of her lunch, secured it in the pack, and flung it on her back. "I want to follow while the scent is hot."

Amie scampered to her feet. "Here we go again."

Landy brought Belle back to the shoreline, where once again her ears perked up.

"We can't cross here," Amie cried. "The water's too fast on the other shore."

"Right," Landy said, nodding in agreement. "Let's ride upstream. I think I remember a calmer spot."

The girls mounted their palominos and rode close to the river, trying to find a safe crossing. Each turn seemed to take them to more white water and away from the scent.

The north fork of the Feather River had a dynamic personality. Parts of it wound gently, like a stream, while other areas rushed violently against jagged rocks. Sections seemed bottomless with dark flowing waters, but mostly it was about four feet deep, depending on the year's snow runoff.

Finally, Landy spied a clearing where a crossing was possible. "Let's cross here," she said.

"I don't know," Amie said, slowly. "It looks pretty deep to me."

"Not really," Landy said. "I can see the bottom. It's not too rocky, and the water's not running fast. Come on, Amie, we've already gone upstream about a quarter of a mile. This is as good as it's going to get."

Amie sighed. "I suppose you're right, but that doesn't mean I have to like it."

Landy grasped the reins a little tighter and gently nudged Belle into the water. The runoff was high, reaching about hock level on the horses.

Landy could feel the spray of cold water splash

her arms and face. Belle's steps were small, yet sure. The river was only about fifteen feet wide, and the far side was calm with no rocky bottom.

Suddenly Amie screamed. "My bag!" she cried.

The small canvas bag in which Amie had been gathering her flowers was floating downstream.

Landy reached back and out across the river, but the bag was several feet away from her grasp. "Are you okay?" she called back to Amie.

"Yes," Amie said. "We left in such a hurry I didn't tie the bag very well and it slipped off."

"When we're across, we can look for it. It may have washed up on shore or gotten tangled in the bushes." Landy raised the reins again and squeezed her ankles on Belle's sides. A few steps later and Landy had finished the crossing. Belle whinnied and shook off the cold water from her protective hair.

Amie followed closely behind. "I really liked that bag."

"We'll find it," Landy said sympathetically.

Within minutes the girls had traveled through the fields of wildflowers and long grass past their picnic spot. Both riders kept close to the river's edge, searching for the canvas bag. With the current running so fast, Landy now wondered if they would find the treasured bag.

"Whoa, girl," Landy whispered, pulling back on the reins. About a hundred yards from their picnic spot, Landy spied a man and woman hunched by the riverbank.

"Who do you think they are?" Amie asked.

"I'll bet they're the brother and sister staying at the Tremanes' resort," Landy said.

"Maybe we should leave them alone," Amie said.

"I'm going to go over and introduce myself," Landy said. "Maybe they saw your bag come by."

Cautiously, Landy approached the couple. Within a few feet she noticed Amie's soaked canvas bag sitting in the long grass on the shore.

Just then Belle let out a long whinny as if to announce her arrival, startling the couple.

"Whoa," the man said, looking over his shoulder. The ridge of the bank was just steep enough for him to lose his balance, and he stepped directly into a pool section of the river. His partner quickly extended her hand and caught him, keeping him from toppling over into the current.

"I'm sorry," Landy apologized. "We didn't mean to startle you." She quickly dismounted. "My name's Landy Berensen, and this is my horse, Belle."

Amie joined them. "And I'm Amie Clark and this is Copper."

"Nice to meet you," the man said, stomping his wet boots on dry land. "My name's Will Evans and this is my sister Amanda."

"My horse picked up your scent and led us over," Landy explained, while tying Belle's reins to a nearby ponderosa pine tree.

"I'm a historian and Amanda's a geologist," Will began. "We're here for a couple of weeks studying some of the area's gold rush legends."

Amie dismounted and let Copper drink from the river. "My bag!" she exclaimed.

"Ah, so that belongs to you," Amanda said.

"It came floating by a few minutes ago," Will added.

Amanda made a notation in her journal before setting it into her knapsack. "We wondered if there might be a couple of prospectors panning for gold."

Landy knew they were teasing her. "There hasn't been any gold discovered in this area for years."

"Don't be so hasty," Will said.

"There are probably a lot of small veins around," Amanda said. "Nothing to warrant an investment by a large company, but there's definitely 'gold in them thar hills'."

Amie sat on the trunk of a large tree and began taking her flowers out to dry them in the sun. Landy perched on a rock, and Amanda and Will nestled into the lawn chairs they'd set up in the grass.

"Have you ever heard of a miner named Thomas Robertson Stoddart?" Amanda asked.

Landy shrugged. "I don't think I paid attention that day in school."

Will laughed. "According to the legend, Stoddart and a companion became lost in the mountains. Exhausted and desperate, they came to a lake surrounded by three high peaks. They were thirsty, so they went to drink the cold, clear water of the lake. They discovered that the shores and bottom were studded with lumps of gold."

"Really?" Landy exclaimed.

"Tell us more," Amie pleaded.

Will smiled. "It was late fall, 1849, too late to set up camp, so they each took a large bag of gold and headed for the mining camps on the Yuba River. Unfortunately, they were ambushed. Stoddart's companion disappeared and was presumed dead, and his gold was never recovered. Some folks think it's still hidden somewhere up in these mountains."

"What about Stoddart?" Landy asked.

"Stoddart eventually made it to the camp, but empty-handed. He claimed to have hidden his share of the gold before being ambushed," Amanda said.

"All winter long it appears Stoddart bragged about the gold," Will said, picking up on the saga. "He had so many different stories going that most folks were skeptical it even existed."

"What about the lake?" Amie inquired.

Amanda rested her elbows on her knees. "One version of the legend says the lake never existed. Another says the lake was discovered on the border of Oregon, reaping millions of dollars for the claim company that discovered it."

She opened up a notebook of Will's, checked his notes, and read from them. "Stoddart led a group of miners out the following spring. He studied the configurations of peaks, twisted trees, and shadows, but couldn't find the lake. When the others in his party started getting restless, Stoddart snuck away in the night, never to be seen again."

"The venture wasn't a total loss, though," Will continued. "A group of Germans who had traveled with Stoddart started back toward Downieville."

Amie pointed to the south. "That's not far from here."

Landy tapped her cowboy hat. "We've ridden in horse shows there."

"The Germans decided to prospect as they went back, taking a very roundabout route." Will leaned

43

forward in his chair. "One miner was carrying water back to their campsite on the east branch of the north fork of Feather River, when he discovered a rock in which every crack was filled with gold."

"Rich Bar," Landy blurted out.

"It was one of the richest claims around," Amie added.

"That's why we're in Caribou this summer," Amanda said. "We're following up on old legends and investigating what historical and geological importance they may have had on California attaining statehood.

"So you're not looking for Stoddart's lake filled with gold?" Landy asked.

"There's not enough factual evidence to justify that," Will said.

"There are lots of deserted mining camps around here," Amie said. "Smith's, Indian's, Peasoup, Muggins."

Landy shrugged her shoulders. "We've gone to most of them on school field trips."

"Well, next time you go, keep your eyes peeled for treasure maps and gold dust," Amanda declared. "You might get rich."

Suddenly, Landy jumped up. "It was very nice meeting you both," she said. "Amie and I have to go now. I hope we see you again soon."

"Yes, thank you for the stories," Amie added, as she rushed to gather her bag and flowers. "What's gotten into you?" she whispered to Landy.

Landy untied both horses in record time, mounted Belle, and headed back up the river. "Bye," she called out.

With Landy in the lead, the girls retraced their steps and made an uneventful crossing of the river.

"So tell me, why did we have to rush off like that?" Amie asked as they passed their picnic spot.

Landy stopped in a grove of trees overlooking the steep, zigzagging roads referred to as switchbacks and looked around to make sure no one was nearby.

"Well?" Amie asked.

Landy could no longer hide her enthusiasm. "I have the solution to all of our money problems."

"What?" Amie said in a half whisper.

"The treasure," Landy said. "We're going to find Stoddart's lost treasure."

The Legend

66 There's no reason we can't find that gold," Landy explained, as the girls finished cooling down their horses back at the Berensens'. They had talked about the possibilities of finding gold during the ride home. Landy and Amie had unsaddled the horses, walked, watered, and groomed them. Now with the last carrot gobbled, Landy sent Belle into the pasture.

Claire Berensen called from the front porch, "Landy, I'm driving into town with Jason in a few minutes. Do you and Amie want to come along?"

Landy turned to Amie. "I'll make you a deal. We go into town with my mom, spend some time at the library, and see if there is any truth to the Stoddart legend."

"Then what?" Amie questioned.

"If it looks like there's any truth to the legend, we go for it."

"I'm afraid it's going to be a waste of time," Amie said, as they walked toward the house.

"Trust me," Landy said. "I'll go tell my mom we're going."

A little while later the girls were climbing the steps to the Caribou public library. It wasn't a modern building, but a large, old Victorian house built by a wealthy family in the early 1900s.

With the information that Amanda and Will had given them, the girls were able to find many references to Stoddart, Rich Bar, and the lake of gold.

"The lake of gold is definitely out," Landy declared.

Amie agreed. "I don't think it ever existed."

"We've been to Rich Bar, and I'm pretty sure it has been stripped of every nugget or dust speck," Landy said. "So that leaves the rest of the Stoddart legend."

Landy leaned over two books the girls had placed on the oak table. "Look at that," she said, pointing to a copy of a black–and–white pencil drawing.

"What about it?" Amie asked.

"It says it's the spot by the Feather River where Stoddart was ambushed," Landy said.

Amie raised her eyebrows and stared at her

friend. "The Feather River is very big, you know."

Landy tapped the picture. "Look at the twisted tree."

"It looks like the Big Meadow," Amie said.

"Exactly," Landy said. She flipped a few more pages. "And here is the drawing of the camp they left from."

"That could be anywhere from Downieville to Oregon."

Landy picked up another book. "Look what it says here," she said, reading from it. "'During the long winter at the Yuba River camp, Stoddart would regale his friends with stories of the gold he had found, often drawing maps to elaborate.'" Landy let out a scream of excitement.

All eyes turned in her direction, and a series of "shhs" and "quiet pleases" bombarded the otherwise silent room.

Landy and Amie covered their mouths to muffle the giggles. "Don't you see the importance of this?" Landy asked.

"Not really," Amie admitted.

"There's a map, maybe many maps, telling of the spot where they were ambushed. Didn't the legend say that his partner disappeared, and his gold was never recovered?"

"Yes," Amie said excitedly.

"Who knows? Maybe that gold is still out there and Stoddart's too—just waiting for someone to find. Let's make copies of the sketches to use as reference."

"Hi, Landy, Amie," came a familiar voice from behind them.

Landy and Amie looked up in surprise to find Monica Tremane with a smug smile on her lips.

"Oh, hi, Monica," Landy replied. "What are you doing here?"

Monica leaned over the table to check out the books the girls were investigating. "I help out at the library as a volunteer."

Landy frantically closed the books, pulled them closer to her, and grabbed two more at random from the shelves. If there was anyone she didn't want to know her plans to search for gold, it was Monica Tremane.

"Perhaps I can help you locate something," Monica said. She leaned over and picked up the top book from the stack. "Fairies? What do you want to learn about fairies?"

Landy's eyes widened. "Fairies, well," she said with a laugh. "Costumes. We're trying to get ideas for our costumes for the horse show." Landy quickly slipped the three volumes about the gold rush to the floor under the table so Monica couldn't see them.

"You're thinking about going as fairies?" Monica asked.

"We're keeping our options open, checking every possibility," Amie said.

"What do fairies and palominos have in common?" Monica asked.

"That's it, nothing," Landy said. "That's why we burst out laughing. Fairies and palominos, pretty ridiculous, huh?"

"I think so," Monica said.

"Well, thanks for stopping by," Landy said, smiling sweetly. She and Amie sat with their arms crossed on the table, staring at Monica until she walked away.

"That was close," Landy said.

"I can't believe you told her we were going to the horse show as fairies."

"Hey, I grabbed the first books on the shelf," Landy said. "The other one isn't any better. Look, it's about witches."

Amie picked up the gold rush books from under the table. "I'll go copy the pages, while you see if any of these other books have maps or charts."

"Good plan," Landy said. She took the books and sat facing the door. If Monica returned, she would be able to spot her immediately. The first volume had crude, handmade sketches of miners' maps with old camp sites and cities x-ed in. The second was easier to read and also had some familiar landmarks from around Caribou. Landy stared at a map showing three peaks and a cliff.

"What's with the gold digger stuff?" Jason Berensen asked.

Landy jumped in surprise. She flattened her body out over the map. "Costumes," Landy blurted. "Costume plans for the horse parade."

"What are you going as," Jason asked with a snicker, "a map of California?"

Jason was a tall, lanky thirteen-year-old. He had the same blonde hair as Landy, but blue eyes like their mother's, not hazel like Landy's and their dad's. Jason and Landy had good days when they got along, but there were also days when his teasing was relentless, and everything they did got on each other's nerves.

"The maps are just ideas," Landy insisted.

"Yeah, ideas about finding gold. I heard you and Amie whispering about geologists and gold," Jason said. "I also know you need two hundred dollars quick."

"Okay, so what if we are looking for gold? Nobody's asking you to help," Landy snapped.

Jason paused for a minute, staring at his sister.

"You're crazy. No one has found gold in this area for years."

"Well, maybe they just didn't know where to look," Landy said.

Jason rolled his eyes. "And you do?"

"Maybe," Landy said. "What did you come in here for anyway?"

"Mom told me to tell you two to wrap it up. It's late and we're leaving in ten minutes."

"We'll be right out." She grabbed the book and walked away, her confidence shaken. She knew Jason was probably right about the gold, but there seemed to be enough evidence to warrant a search. She had to at least try.

Landy found Amie at the copy machine, and copied the two maps she'd found as well. When she turned to put the books away, Jason was there.

"We'll be there in a minute," Landy whispered.

"Look, I think your whole idea is crazy, but I might be able to help."

"Why would you want to help us?" Landy asked suspiciously.

"I'm your brother."

"I'll ask again, why would you want to help?" Landy held tightly onto the books.

"Call it curiosity," Jason said. "I didn't get a very

good look at that map you were checking out, but I might know one of the landmarks."

Landy and Amie exchanged glances. Landy held firm, but Amie seemed to soften. "It's okay with me," she whispered.

"I promise not to tell anyone," he said.

"Okay," Landy said, reluctantly, "but no laughing." She cautiously set the book on the nearest table and flipped to the page with the three peaks. Then she opened the second volume to the page with the miners' camp.

Jason pressed his index finger on the miners' camp and dragged it across to the three peaks map. Then he tapped the miner's camp. "I think I know where that is," he said.

"You're not just teasing us, are you?" Landy asked.

"I once rode up there with Dad during the rainy season. You can't get there by car, so groups stay away. It's not part of the hiking trails either. The national forest hasn't even opened it to the public."

"That's supposed to be the place where Stoddart spent the winter before going to look for the lake of gold. They say he drew plans and maps of his claim," Landy said.

"It's kind of a tough ride to describe," Jason said, scratching his head.

"Would you take us?" Landy begged.

"Please," Amie said.

"I'll do anything," Landy pleaded. "I'll pick up your room or clean out Apache's stall. Please take us there."

Jason sighed. "It's too late to go today and tomorrow it's supposed to rain and thunder."

"What about the next day, then?" Landy asked.

"I'm working at the tree farm with Dad. I promised him I'd be there by noon."

"We could go in the morning," Landy urged.

"I guess I could take you early in the morning," Jason said.

"Thanks, Jason. You're the best brother in the whole world."

"I'm not promising anything," Jason said. "I can just take you there. Then I've got to meet Dad."

"That's all we ask," Landy said.

The trio met Mrs. Berensen at the car. Landy was practically floating with excitement. She explained that Jason wanted to take them to the old deserted mining camp in two days. Both girls promised they'd be careful.

When they got home, Landy got out her compass, binoculars, and rain poncho in preparation for the big day. "Amie, do you realize all the incredible things we'll be able to get when we find the gold?"

"It should be enough to pay for our registration fee," Amie said.

"Didn't you read about the thousands of dollars some of the prospectors took out of the mines?" Landy asked.

Amie helped Landy pack supplies for Thursday's ride. "I'd settle for the registration fee and a fabulous costume."

"We'll have enough for the registration fee, costumes, saddles, bridles, and maybe even an air-conditioned horse trailer like Monica's."

"We're not setting up a claim, Landy," Amie reminded her.

"We've got to work fast," Landy said. She stuffed her supplies into her backpack. "We've got to find the gold before the registration fee is due. We just have to."

Golden Opportunities

On Thursday, dressed in denim jeans, boots, her lucky sweatshirt, leather gloves, and a straw cowboy hat, Landy saddled Belle. The day before there had been a heavy thunderstorm, but today the sky was streaked with pinks and purples, replacing the dark shadows and grays of the day before.

It was shortly after dawn, and Landy had hardly slept a wink. She was so excited about the gold hunt that she'd tossed and turned, thinking of all the riches she could find.

"You don't want to forget this," Jason said. He handed Landy a canteen of water, which she secured to the saddle.

Landy filled her lungs with crisp, clean air. Her skin tingled with anticipation. Her jean jacket felt good against the morning cold, but she knew by the time they reached the mine, the weather would be hot.

Landy stuck her foot in the stirrup and swung her other leg up and over the saddle. "I'm going to ride ahead to Amie's house," she told Jason. "I'll meet you there."

Within twenty minutes, the threesome was on its way up a path near the Feather River. The birds were flitting around looking for food, tracks from the night animals still marked the riverbank, and the dew on the wildflowers had not yet dried in the sun.

"This is where we take our first turn," Jason announced. "Let's stop for a water break."

The path was marked with a large rock formation, which locals had tagged Paul Bunyan's boot. It looked like the sole of a hiking boot that even included a big hole just below the big toe.

After their break, the three followed a path that led into thicker brush and denser trees. There were times when Landy could hardly see the sun, and the air felt cool and damp. She ducked and pushed away branches from her face, glad Belle wasn't afraid or skittish. Landy turned in her saddle to check on how

Copper and Amie were doing.

"No wonder people don't come this way much," Amie said. "It's kind of creepy."

Unexpectedly, Jason stopped. "We've got a problem up here." He pulled over to the edge of the path, leaving a space for Belle and Landy to move into. A large, fallen tree blocked their way.

Landy squinted into the forest, "It must have fallen in yesterday's thunderstorm."

"So what do we do now?" Amie asked.

"Well, as I see it, we have two choices," Jason began. "We can turn back and forget the whole thing, or . . ."

"Move the tree," Landy interrupted. "I've got a rope. Maybe Belle and I can pull the top part of the tree far enough away to let us pass."

The tree was a large pine. Its trunk lay uprooted about twenty feet back into the forest. The portion that blocked the path wasn't too thick, but its branches hoisted it above the path about eight feet. Too high to jump, but too low and dense to pass under. It extended past the path and finally topped off another fifteen feet in the opposite direction.

Jason cleared his throat. "Now how exactly are you planning to move this tree?"

"I'm not sure, but if I lead Belle around the top of

the tree, tie the rope around the section blocking the path, and lead Belle along the path, the tree might move."

Amie looked at the steep drop–off where Landy and Belle would attempt to cross. "I wish I could say that Copper would go through that, but I'm having enough trouble encouraging her down the path."

"Apache's not so great at that stuff either," Jason added.

Landy sighed. "So it's up to Belle and me."

"It looks that way, Sis," Jason said. "If it starts getting too dangerous, promise me you'll turn back."

"I promise." Landy dismounted Belle and took out a few carrots from her pocket. She held onto the bridle where it connected to the bit and moved slowly, stomping on as many twigs and branches and as much underbrush as she could.

At first the route wasn't too bad, a little slippery with dew, but not too steep. Then Landy saw the drop. The top of the tree extended out over a steep embankment. "Easy, girl," Landy whispered. Landy could feel her legs shake with the strain. Her whole body wanted to lurch forward, and it took a lot of effort not to fall. She could tell Belle was also feeling the strain.

Suddenly Landy's feet skidded out from under her

without any warning. Her boots flew up in front of her, while her back headed for the dirt. As Landy's back slammed into the moist dirt, she grabbed onto some branches and held on. Then, twisting her body to face the dirt, she crawled up the slope on her hands and knees until she reached Belle.

"Are you all right?" Jason called to his sister.

"Yes," Landy replied.

She and Belle continued. Now they had to go up the embankment, and Belle grunted as she dug her hooves into the loose dirt.

When they reached the top of the embankment, Landy quickly urged Belle around the tip of the tree. As horse and rider emerged on the other side of the path, Landy called out, "We made it!"

"I've knotted your rope around the trunk," Jason said. "As soon as you think Belle is ready, give it a try."

Landy nodded as she tied the rope around her saddle horn. She mounted Belle and they walked out until the rope was pulled taut. "Here we go," Landy called over her shoulder.

At first there was no movement; the tree was just too big and too set to move. Jason and Amie tried prying some of the buried branches loose, as well as kicking and breaking others that might be keeping it from moving. On the next attempt the tree budged an inch or so.

Landy gently kicked Belle, encouraging her to pull ahead, as Jason and Amie gave cheers of support. Slowly the tree moved from its spot, creating an opening like a door swinging on its hinges. At last the path was wide enough for the others to pass.

"How much farther?" Landy asked when the others had joined her.

"At least another two miles," Jason said.

They continued past Castle Rock, a beautiful formation of limestone and shale. They traveled over an old wooden bridge and followed some gentle switchbacks to an opening above the area known as Big Meadow.

The midmorning sun shone brightly, and the team gladly shed their jean jackets. After a final incline, they arrived at the remnants of the deserted mining village.

"We made it," Landy cheered.

"At last," Amie said.

Jason jumped off Apache. "Let's start looking."

The girls tied the horses to the remains of an old hitching post.

"I'm going to look over there," Amie said, pointing to a dilapidated, three-walled structure.

Landy began pulling back the overgrown grass by the foundation of another structure. "It doesn't look like anyone's been here for years."

"It's no wonder," Jason said. "It's not that great a spot for sightseeing as far as deserted mining towns go."

"That's because other people don't know there might be a treasure map hidden here," Landy said.

"I'm running out of time," Jason said, looking at his watch. "Let's split up, so we won't be hunting where someone has already searched."

The girls nodded in agreement. Jason gave out the assignments. "I'll see if there is anything over by that grove of trees. Amie, why don't you take a look by that smaller cabin, and Landy check out the remains of the Long Tom."

The Long Tom was a series of long boxes with strainers. The miners shoveled dirt that they hoped contained gold into the boxes. There was a constant flow of water that turned the dirt into mud. The mud was stirred and washed through the strainers, leaving the gold to be plucked out by the excited miner. Now, the boxes were mostly rotted out planks leaning next to the rocks that had once held them up off the ground.

"Doesn't look like much," Landy said. She lifted a

few rusted pipes only to reveal homes and hiding places for bugs. "It's hard to believe that hundreds of people lived up here and found their fortunes."

"Fortunes," Jason said with a snort. "Most of the prospectors didn't strike it rich. They were lucky if they got back to their homes or were able to start some new businesses here in California."

Landy refused to have her gold rush spirit dampened. "Will and Amanda said there was still plenty of gold here. Besides, we're not looking to start a mine, we're just hoping to find something someone lost."

"Over a hundred years ago," Amie said softly.

Landy chucked a few more rusted pipes into a pile. They'd probably been used to carry water from the river to the Long Tom. She carefully inspected each pipe before discarding it.

Then she spied a small, rusty cylinder partially buried in the ground. She clawed at the gravel and dug into the dirt to help loosen it. Then after lifting it carefully from its resting place, she removed her gloves and used her index finger to feel a small, tightly wound piece of paper protected inside.

"I've found something!" Landy shouted.

Amie and Jason rushed over.

"What is it?" Jason asked.

Landy tugged ever so lightly on the material, and a rectangular shaped piece of paper emerged from inside.

"It's a map," Amie whispered.

With her hands shaking like the leaves on an aspen tree, Landy unrolled the yellowed piece of parchment delicately, trying not to destroy the contents. The drawing was faint, but with Jason's help the girls deciphered the dotted lines.

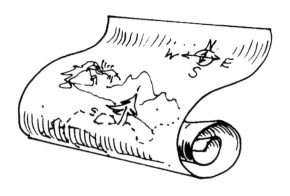

Landy gasped. "It looks old. I bet it . . . "

Jason interrupted her. "I'm sorry, guys, but I can't stay. I promised Dad I'd help him work at the farm."

"How can you think about working at the tree farm at a time like this?" Landy asked.

"It's not my first choice either, but Dad's depending on me," Jason said. "I'm going to be late as it is."

"But if you discovered gold, he'd understand why you didn't show up."

"*If* is the main word. If you find gold. If I told Dad we spent all day looking for treasure that we never found, he'd ground me for sure."

"I can't believe you're actually leaving us," Landy said.

Jason untied Apache's reins. "I should have left half an hour ago." He mounted Apache. "And remember, if you find any gold, I'm charging you a finder's fee, so I can be rich, too." He waved to the girls and headed toward the path.

"If we find the gold, we'll show Mom and Dad together," Landy called after him.

"Good luck," Jason said as he galloped down the path.

Landy watched the dust settle as her brother rode out of sight. "Not *if* we find the gold," she whispered, correcting herself, "*when* we find the gold."

Gold Fever

"**I** think we've been to some of these places on school trips," Amie said, looking up from the map.

Landy turned away from the road and walked over to where Amie was crouched beside a large rock.

"This has got to be Chimney Rock," Amie said.

Landy tapped the northwest corner of the map. "And if that isn't Turtle Rock, I'll eat my hat."

"It looks like we start by going back the way we came," Amie said.

"But we don't cross the wooden bridge."

"You're right," Amie said. "Instead we follow the path to the left."

Landy tapped the x marked on the map.

"Ultimately ending at the cave by the twisted tree."

"Look, Stoddart even marked how many paces it is from the tree to the cave," Amie said.

"We should go northeast."

"This is strange." Amie pointed to the drawing of the twisted tree on the map. "I know I've seen that tree somewhere before."

"We've seen many of these sights before, but now we're going to see them through new eyes."

"There are so many caves up there," Amie said with a sigh.

Landy nodded. "And we'll go into all of them until we find the gold."

The girls started the trek toward the wooden bridge. The terrain began to change dramatically. The path got rockier; there was less undergrowth.

Along the way, the girls passed a few caves, none containing anything other than empty soda pop cans, but Landy was determined to check each one.

"Here's another cave," Landy called to Amie. "Belle seems to think this is it."

"This is the third time Belle has led us off the trail," Amie said. "Her curiosity is wearing me out."

"The landscape has changed over the past hundred years. We should check out all the caves we come across."

"That could take weeks."

"Belle led us to Will and Amanda," Landy said. "She has great instincts. Who knows, maybe she has a nose for gold, too."

After a few hours of reaching dead ends, the girls still hadn't found any landmarks from the map. Hungry, they took a break near one of the caves to eat their lunch.

"I wonder if we should have followed the other fork," Amie said through bites of her sandwich.

"It wasn't marked on the map," Landy said.

"Neither were half of the caves we've been into so far," Amie snapped.

"I don't think it's smart to pass them up," Landy insisted.

"Look around," Amie said, "we're heading back to the grasslands. There aren't going to be any more caves to investigate if we keep going this way. Gem Lake is only about a mile away."

Landy stared at Amie. "I think you're wrong."

"Well, I think you're wrong."

The girls ate silently for a while. Landy hated it when they disagreed. Amie was her best friend, but sometimes she could be so difficult. Landy walked away from the lunch spot, stepped on a rock, and peered through the binoculars.

She scanned the horizon to the left and saw nothing. Then she focused on a mound to the right. After making a few adjustments, she called to Amie. "Amie, come here."

Amie groaned. "Did you find another cave?"

"Set your canteen down and come look," Landy commanded.

Reluctantly, Amie sauntered over to Landy. "What now?"

Landy took the binoculars' strap from around her neck, and placed it around Amie's. "Look over there and tell me what you see."

Amie sighed and rolled her eyes. "Maybe we should think about giving horse rides again."

"Stop moaning and look," Landy said. She positioned Amie in the exact spot where she'd been standing.

"I don't see anything but a bunch of grass."

"Not there. Beyond the grass."

Amie refocused the binoculars. "I see rocks stacked up or something."

"Stacked rocks, Chimney Rock. Remember the map had a place marked Chimney Rock?"

"Oh, Landy, I think you're right. They don't look very big, but there are three of them, just like on the map."

"I'm sorry I snapped at you before," Landy said. "I should have listened to you when you said to take the other fork."

Quickly they stuffed their lunch leftovers into their saddlebags and rode back to the fork. Within a few yards the terrain changed drastically from an open field to a steady incline of ledges. Cautiously, they followed a narrow path long overgrown with grass and weeds.

The girls arrived at the base of the stack of rocks and dismounted. "They're not very big," Landy said quietly.

They looked at the map, took out the compass, and walked to the west. Landy's heart pounded with each step.

"There's nothing here," Amie said softly.

Landy turned around. "We have to look closer."

"It looks like a bunch of scraggly sage and evergreen bushes," Amie said.

Landy scrambled up another rock formation. From there she leapt to another rock. "I thought maybe I could see something from higher ground, but it's a big zero." Landy squatted and peered back the way she'd come. She cocked her head and smiled. "Hey," she exclaimed. "Behind you. There's a big rock with a small crack on one side."

"It's in the opposite direction from the map," Amie said.

"So Stoddart had a terrible sense of direction." Landy climbed down from her perch. She got a flashlight from her saddlebag, flicked it on, and peered into the two-by-three foot slit in the rock.

"Are you going in?" Amie asked.

"I think I have to. This is the closest we've gotten to anything on the map."

Amie winced. "I hope there aren't any animals inside."

Landy shined her flashlight again just to be sure.

"I think the bottom is a few feet down," Landy reported. She dropped a pebble in and waited for it to hit. "At least it's solid ground and not water."

She untied the rope from her saddle and secured one end around the saddle horn. "I'm going to need your help again, girl," she whispered to Belle.

Landy tied the rope around her waist using a bowline knot. She clipped the flashlight to her belt loop and set her cowboy hat on the saddle. "I'm not sure how far it is to the bottom, but by the sound of the rock, it couldn't be more than a few feet. I think I can drop down, but you might have Belle stand ready to pull me out if it's farther than I think."

"I'm scared," Amie whispered.

"Me too," Landy admitted. "I'm excited too, though. This could be the answer to everything." Eagerly, Landy climbed back to the opening and prepared to drop into the unknown.

The opening was small and Landy shimmied through. With Belle keeping the rope taut she slipped over the edge. To her pleasant surprise, she landed at the bottom of the chamber four feet below.

"Are you all right?" Amie called down.

Landy strained to look at her surroundings, but her eyes hadn't made the adjustment to the dark. "So far so good." Landy squatted down and shone the light in front of her. The rock slanted from the opening to a three-foot ceiling and a back wall about six feet away. The cold rocks, musty air, and dark interior didn't feel very friendly.

Landy crawled on her hands and knees around the perimeter of the small pit. Shining her flashlight, she discovered a lump near the back wall. "There's something in here," she called back to Amie, who was now crouched at the opening.

Landy tried digging around the base of the lump with her gloved hands, but she couldn't loosen the object or figure out what it was. She tried kicking it with her boots, and although some of the dirt fell off, it didn't shift.

Landy decided to try something different. She took the rope from her waist and tied it around the base of the mound as securely as possible.

"How's it going?" Amie called.

"Fine. Walk Belle away from the cave," Landy instructed Amie.

Within moments the rope strands squeaked, pulled rigid, and the mound shifted. Some of the encrusted dirt fell away, revealing a rectangular shape.

"Stop," Landy called. She dug around the base again and tried to lift the object, but with the low ceiling and heavy weight, it wouldn't budge.

"Okay, go slowly," Landy called. She crawled to the back of the object, and, lying on her back, positioned her feet to push it up through the tunnel.

Between her pushing and Belle's pulling, the object was unearthed. With an extra push from Landy, it skidded across the dirt floor.

Landy poked her head through the cave's opening. "The next part's going to be tough," she said.

"Can you tell what it is yet?" Amie asked excitedly.

"It's some kind of box."

"Can you lift it?"

"No, it's too heavy, and the ledge of this wall is too high. Take some carrots and hold them in front of

Belle's nose. She'd lift a piano to get her favorite treat."

Amie laughed. "If this works, I'll never tease you again about carrying those things around."

The weight was heavy, and Belle felt the strain, but as Landy said, she'd go a long way for a few carrots. As Amie prodded Belle, Landy used her shoulder to push the box up the jagged wall. With one last heave the partners boosted the box, and it tumbled onto the rocky terrain and into the sunlight.

Landy found a few footholds and climbed out to examine the treasure.

"This is the most exciting thing that has ever happened to me," Amie said.

"Until we win the parade contest," Landy said. "Let's get the rest of this dirt off and find out what exactly this thing is."

The girls scraped off years of mud, rock, and dirt from the box.

Landy buffed a corner with her glove. "Look, if you rub this part, it shines."

The two girls worked in silence under the strong glare of the summer sun. Then Landy stopped working. "I think it's some kind of a strongbox. You can see there used to be a lock on the outside."

"Wait a minute. Stoddart didn't say anything

about having a chest," Amie said.

"Who cares," Landy said, rubbing the box harder with her glove. "It must have carried something valuable."

Amie dug her fingers into a small opening. "Maybe we can pry the lid section loose."

With their hearts pounding and adrenaline racing through their bodies, the girls maneuvered their fingers between the top and the bottom and lifted the lid.

"We're rich," Landy whispered, as the lid was swung open. Then she peered inside.

The chest was empty.

Last Chances

"Where's the gold?" Landy cried. She lifted the edge of the chest, hoping to see gold nuggets or at least gold dust.

Amie sat back in the dirt, resting her arms on bent knees. "Maybe there's a false bottom or a hidden section."

Landy frantically kept looking. "Nothing," she reported at last. She stood up. "I can't believe this."

Amie picked up a clump of dry dirt and tossed it back down. "How can there be a treasure chest and no treasure?"

Landy brushed the dust and dirt from her jeans. "Maybe it's still in the cave." She grabbed her flashlight and ran back to the entrance. This time she didn't use a rope, but quickly dropped to the floor and crawled to the spot where she'd moved the chest. Desperately, she clawed the area for signs of gold. She emerged empty-handed.

Amie met her at the entrance. "Anything?"

"Zip," Landy answered. She felt so let down she wanted to cry. They'd worked so hard, how could they have come up with nothing? Was Stoddart just a crazy man with wild stories? If the map was real, why wasn't there any gold? "Let's take a look at the map again," she said.

"What for?" Amie replied glumly.

Landy marched past her to the horses. "You're not ready to give up, are you?"

"I don't know," Amie said. She sat on a rock. "It just seems so hopeless."

"You didn't feel that way when we found the chest."

Landy took the map from her saddlebag and mentally retraced their steps. "We're on the right track," she said, pointing to Chimney Rock. "Chimney Rock is on the map, but that's not the spot Stoddart marked. Remember, the gold is at the twisted tree, not Chimney Rock."

The girls climbed to the highest point around and

used the binoculars to search for the twisted tree. "The twisted tree on the map looks so close to Chimney Rock. Why can't we see it?" Amie asked. "What if the tree died, or was chopped down, or was hit by lightning?"

Landy noticed that Belle had wandered to the edge of the path. "You're not ready to give up, are you, girl? See, Amie, Belle thinks we should keep going this way."

Amie shrugged and sighed. "Her guess is as good as any."

"We need to stick to the map," Landy said. "I promise I won't stop to look in any more caves unless they have a twisted tree nearby. Deal?"

"Deal," Amie answered.

With renewed enthusiasm, the girls repacked their supplies and continued on a northwest route. Three bends later, there was still no sign of a twisted tree.

They pressed on until they reached another fork in the road. After examining the map, they decided to go left.

Within fifty feet, Landy suddenly stood up in her stirrups. "Look," she said. "Over there." She pointed to the base of a very twisted and gnarly ponderosa pine.

Amie let out a scream of delight. Then she rode alongside of Belle, and the girls exchanged high-fives.

The girls rode up to a series of rocks where a massive tree stood sentry. "Grab the compass," Landy said. She grasped the map, dismounted, and kissed Belle's nose. "This time we've found the real thing."

"Okay, what do we do?" Amie asked.

"We mark off twenty-five paces to the east."

"Do you see a cave?" Amie asked.

"Not yet. I'll bet it's hidden."

The girls linked arms and prepared to mark off twenty-five paces. Amie hesitated. "What if Stoddart's paces were bigger than ours? Even if he was a short man, we should take big steps."

"Now you're thinking," Landy said.

The girls looked at each other and squeezed each other's arms in excitement. "Ready," Landy began.

"Set, go," they added together.

Taking giant-sized steps, the girls marched twenty-five paces to the east. When they completed the task, they found themselves facing a pile of broken branches.

"Do you see a cave?" Amie asked.

"No," Landy said, unlinking arms. She stuck her hands into the branches to see if there was anything behind them. "Ouch," she cried, pulling her hand back. "Those branches are prickly." She took the gloves from her belt, put them on, and slid her jean jacket over the top of her arm. Now she was covered from neck to fingertips.

Landy's second attempt went much easier. "Hey, some of these branches are loose," she said. She grabbed a large branch and tossed it behind her. The branches were dense and prickly, but Landy and Amie successfully moved them to reveal a couple of sage bushes covering the entrance to a cave.

"I've got the butterflies again," Amie said.

Landy couldn't speak and nodded her agreement. "Flashlights," she finally said.

The girls left the horses by the twisted tree, grabbed their flashlights, and peered through the bushes to the cave's interior.

Amie took a step backwards. "You don't think there are any bodies in there, do you?"

"Anything's possible," Landy replied.

Amie stepped back farther from the entrance. "What about Stoddart? Was he ever found?"

"No," Landy said. "He disappeared without a trace and so did his gold. Now you can stand guard if you want, but I'm going in."

Amie took a deep breath. "I'm going in, too."

"Let's go then." Pulling back the sage branches, they stepped through the cave's opening side by side.

Inside it was cool but dry. The girls blinked until

their eyes adjusted to the darkness.

"This is the biggest cave yet," Landy said, shining her light on the curved walls and high rock ceiling.

Amie pointed her flashlight to the center of the cave. "Someone has been in here," she said, as she crouched down and poked at the remnants of a campfire.

The rear of the cave was marred with black streaks. "The walls are charred with smoke," Landy said.

The girls split up and continued their search in opposite directions. All they uncovered were piles of dirt and sticks.

Unexpectedly, a noise by the entrance startled them. Amie dropped her flashlight and ran to Landy, who shut off her beam. The two huddled by the rear wall waiting for the next sound. The light from Amie's flashlight danced on the cave walls, creating shadows and designs.

A large shadow at the entrance of the cave moved slowly toward them. Landy's mind raced with thoughts of a thousand scenarios. Had someone followed them? Was it a bear or other wild creature? Or were they in the home of a hermit?

A sound reverberated in the chamber. The girls ducked down. Amie began to cry. Landy held her tighter. What kind of animal was she going to have to face? The sound was oddly familiar, yet different somehow. Then her shoulders relaxed, and she released her grip on Amie.

"Belle, is that you?" Landy asked. She crawled to Amie's illuminated flashlight and pointed it at the entrance. There, standing in the shadows behind the sage bushes, was Belle. "I don't know whether to hug you or scold you," she cried. "It's Belle," Landy called back to Amie. "I can't believe she came in here. I guess we were so excited about finding the cave, we forgot to tie up the horses. Do you think Copper's okay?"

Amie wiped the tears from her face. "There was a lot of grass to nibble on, so she'll be busy for a while. She's not as curious as Belle."

"Grab my flashlight and we'll go tie them up," Landy said.

Amie picked up the flashlight from the dirt floor. "I thought we were goners there for a minute."

"Me too," Landy said. She walked over to where Belle blocked the entrance and slid her hand around the bridle.

In Belle's mouth was a flimsy, ragged piece of burlap. "Now what have you found?" Landy asked.

Pressing the flashlight between her side and elbow, she attempted to remove the cloth. "Where did you find this?"

Amie came over to help her, but as Landy struggled with the material, her light flashed on something on the dirt floor. It reflected back up at the girls. Landy dropped the burlap and shone the light on the cave floor. Once again it twinkled in the darkness. Landy gasped, as she refocused on the glittering pile. "Gold!" she cried out. "It's gold!"

CHAPTER NINE

Striking It Rich

"We're rich," Landy said. "Rich." The girls stared at each other, stunned.

"You did it, girl," Landy said, hugging Belle. "You led us right to the gold."

The girls sat on the ground and each picked up a nugget.

"Look how big it is," Amie whispered.

Landy was practically hypnotized. "It actually sparkles." The light from outside the cave danced on the glistening specks embedded in chunks of stone.

The girls began stuffing their pockets with gold.

"Just think how long it's been sitting in here, waiting for us to find it," Landy said.

"I'm glad Stoddart wasn't huddled beside it, though," Amie admitted.

"I'll bet he hid it here before he was ambushed and planned to come back for it when it was safe," Landy said. She grabbed two handfuls of nuggets and began filling the saddlebag.

Amie's pockets were full now, too, so she helped Landy load the bag.

Landy stood over the pile. "You know, we prepared pretty well for this expedition, except for one thing."

"What's that?" Amie asked.

"We didn't bring anything in which to put the gold. Our saddlebag is filled with so much of our other stuff, there's hardly any room for the gold."

"Should we leave some behind?" Amie asked. "We can always come back for it later."

"I'm not leaving one speck of gold dust lying on this cave floor."

Amie looked around the cave. "What we need is some kind of box."

Landy's eyes brightened. "And we've got one, too."

"What are you talking about? We didn't bring a box."

"No, but we found one," Landy said. "The strongbox, remember—in the other cave."

Landy led Belle out into the sunshine and unbuckled the saddlebag. She emptied her pockets, and unloaded the other equipment they'd packed for the trip. "I'll take the rope and go back and get the chest. You wait here and guard the treasure."

As she trotted down the path on Belle, Landy's imagination went wild with visions of golden treasure. Her fantasies of winning the parade had faded in the past few days. Now with the discovery of gold, Landy was able to daydream again. She felt light and happy as Belle bounded down the mountain path to the cave by Chimney Rock.

The chest was right where the girls had left it. On her knees, Landy chipped away more debris from the bottom of the box. The encrusted dirt was easier to brush off since it had been drying in the warm afternoon sun. The chest was kind of pretty, Landy decided, in an old rustic way.

Landy rigged the rope around the trunk of a tree. Then she drew the rope over to the saddle, looped it around the saddle horn, and tossed it over a low branch, like a rudimentary pulley system. Very slowly she pulled the end of the rope, and even more slowly it dragged its way through the dirt.

Belle shied at the moving rope. "Easy, girl," Landy said. She tied the rope to a branch and walked to the chest, positioning it at Belle's side.

"This is going to be a little scary," Landy warned her horse. She knew that when she hoisted the chest off the ground, it would swing, creating extra heaviness for Belle.

Landy pulled hard, and as the chest dangled in the air, she wished that Amie could have been there to help her. Taking a deep breath, she pulled again at the heavy weight, raising it higher off the ground. As she had feared, it swung back and forth in between Belle's front and back legs. Belle staggered slightly, grunting.

Landy pulled and pulled until finally she hauled the precious cargo level with the rear rigging portion of the saddle. Once again she tied the rope to the tree and ran back to Belle's side.

"Good girl," she said, giving her horse a pat. She dug deep into her pocket to find two last carrots. Belle eagerly gobbled the treat.

Landy pushed the chest into the seat of the saddle. Carefully she secured the chest and stepped back to admire her work. It was crude, but passable, she decided. After it had been loaded with the gold, she would secure it more.

Because the seat of the saddle was occupied by the chest, Landy positioned herself on the back jockey. She'd ridden there many times when she rode double with Amie.

Cautiously, she and Belle made their journey back to Amie and the gold. It was a much slower trip this time, but Landy didn't mind. She had done what she had set out to do.

As Landy and Belle came up the path, Amie called out, "I'm so glad you're here." She ran up to meet her friend. "A few minutes ago I heard a strange noise in the bushes. I was actually hoping it was some wild animal. I didn't know how I was going to hide gold from a burglar."

Landy laughed, and the girls quickly retied the chest in the center of Belle's saddle. After it was secured, they filled it with the gold. Landy kept one particularly shiny nugget in her hand for good luck.

Landy rode double with Amie on Copper. Slipping Belle's reins over her head, the girls rode in front while Landy held onto the reins and led Belle down the mountainside.

Landy rolled the brilliant nugget over and over in her hand. "For once," she whispered, "Monica Tremane won't be the richest girl in Caribou." Then she leaned forward and tapped Amie on the shoulder. "What are you going to buy first?" she asked.

"After we turn in our registration fee and make

the most incredible costumes in the world, I'll probably put the rest in the bank for college."

"Aren't you going to do anything fun?"

"Well," Amie thought for a moment. "Maybe I'll take a trip to see my cousins in New York. What about you?"

"First, I'm buying a whole new wardrobe. Then I'll get a mountain chalet in Tahoe so we can have a place to go skiing in the wintertime. Next, of course, I'll have to have a beach house in Malibu."

Amie's jaw dropped.

"Do you really think there's that much gold?"

Landy nodded. "Anything's possible."

"Wow!" Amie gasped.

The time passed quickly as the girls joined up to familiar paths that led them back to the Berensens' house. They felt the air cool as the sun made its slow descent in the west.

"Wait until our folks get a load of us," Amie said.

"Jason is going to die when we ride up."

The girls stayed on the high road above town before crossing to the path that led toward home, past the Tremanes' resort.

"Oh, no!" Amie exclaimed. "Look who's ahead of us—Monica Tremane. Let's go another way."

Landy held her breath for a moment. Then she

shook her head. "There is no other way."

"Should we hide until she passes?" Amie asked.

"Too late, she's seen us." Landy slipped off her jean jacket and put it over the chest, tucking the edges of the jacket under the ropes.

"What are you two up to?" Monica asked.

"Be careful," Amie whispered to her friend. "We don't want to spill the beans."

Landy knew she was right, but it would be hard not to let it spill to Monica they had found gold and were rich. "Not much," she told Monica.

"What have you done to poor Belle?" Monica asked. She reached out to take a peek under the jacket, but Landy led Belle away.

"Nothing," Amie said quickly.

"So what's all this other stuff?" Monica said, pressing. She pointed to the saddlebags bulging with flashlights, canteens, and other equipment. "Looks like a lot of junk."

"Trust me, it isn't junk," Landy snapped. "It's treasure."

"Landy," Amie warned.

Monica's eyes grew large. "What kind of treasure?" she asked.

The girls continued riding down the path while Achilles and Monica followed closely.

"You'll find out soon enough," Landy said. "I heard a rumor that there was 'gold in them thar hills'."

"Gold!" Monica exclaimed. "Show me."

"Who said anything about gold?" Amie smiled tensely.

Landy kept up her nonchalant tone. "Some people claim that Caribou is rich in hidden gold."

"You're talking nonsense," Monica stated. "I don't believe a word of it."

"Suit yourself," Landy said. The girls reached the end of the Tremanes' property and kept riding.

Monica abruptly turned Achilles and headed back toward the resort.

As she galloped out of sight, Amie turned to Landy. "Why did you blab to her?"

"I didn't really tell her anything," Landy said.

"Just that we're rich and have gold."

"Amie, everyone in the valley is going to know we have gold in a matter of hours. You can't keep news like this quiet."

Amie snickered. "I could, but it's obvious you can't.

As the pair approached the Berensens' gravel road, the girls could no longer contain their excitement.

"Gold!" Landy shouted.

"We're rich, we're rich," they chanted together.

The porch door swung open, and both girls' families poured out. The Clarks, worried about Amie, had come to the Berensens' to see if their daughter had returned.

"What's going on?" Claire Berensen asked.

Landy slid off the back end of Copper. "We followed the treasure map and found gold, just like the Evanses said." She handed her father the good-luck nugget she'd been holding.

"Now we can go to the horse show in Sacramento," Amie added.

Mrs. Clark covered her mouth. "I can't believe it."

"It's true, really true," Landy said.

Tomas Berensen started to untie the ropes as Landy retrieved her jacket covering the chest.

"There's a ton of it," Landy exclaimed. "It's really heavy and wait until you see how it sparkles."

Landy and Amie told their adventure as they unloaded the chest and carefully set it on the ground. Jason stood nearby, grinning.

"Let's have a look," Tomas Berensen said.

Landy bent down and gently lifted the lid to reveal the rough rocks studded with glitter.

Oohs and ahhs came from all directions. "There's so much," Mr. Clark added. "I wonder why no one ever discovered it until now."

"Who cares?" Landy said. "I'm just glad that it's mine and Amie's."

Tomas Berensen quietly examined the stone Landy gave him, as well as one of the larger ones from the chest. Suddenly, without warning, he slammed the two pieces together with a tremendous force. The stones crumbled in various sizes to the ground.

Landy stared at the broken pieces.

"What happened?" she asked.

"Landy, I'm afraid it's not real," her father said gently, putting his hand on her shoulder. "It's pyrite, more commonly known as fool's gold."

CHAPTER
TEN

Fool's Gold

"**W**hat do you mean, fool's gold?" Landy asked, stunned.

"It can't be," Amie said. "We followed the map."

"Map? What map?" Mrs. Berensen asked.

"The one at the abandoned mine Jason took us to." Landy knelt down and picked up several chunks of the rock. "It was just like the legend said."

Mr. Berensen knelt next to Landy and put his arm around her shoulder.

"Legend or no legend, this gold you've found isn't gold. It just looks like gold."

"You're not alone. Hundreds of miners during the gold rush made the same discovery you have," Mr. Clark said.

"It has to be real," Landy said. She wanted her father to be wrong, but she knew from the look on his face that he was telling the truth. Landy kept shaking her head in disbelief. It was her own fault for getting so wrapped up in her own personal gold rush.

Mr. Clark turned to his daughter. "Amie, tell us again about how you found the gold."

"Fool's gold, you mean," Amie said sadly.

The girls retold their story from the beginning, from their first meeting with Will and Amanda Evans, which led them on their quest for gold. This time the story was told with much less enthusiasm. When Landy reached the part where they uncovered the map, Jason, who had been standing in the background, began to snicker softly. Soon he burst out laughing.

"What's gotten into you?" his mother asked.

Tears were streaming down Jason's face from laughing so much. "You girls fell for it. This was my best joke ever."

His father stood up. "What joke was this?" Mr. Berensen did not sound amused.

Jason stopped laughing. "When the girls were at the library, they were looking at some old legends about the gold rush. I remembered this stash of pyrite my locker partner had from a presentation he had given at school. I thought it might be funny if the girls followed this phony map I planted and found the pyrite instead."

Landy stood up. "You planted the map?"

Jason lowered his head. "When we got to the mine, I slipped it into the pipe. That's why I suggested you look over by the Long Tom."

"And that's why you were so willing to take us up there," Landy said, folding her arms and glaring at him. "And I thought you were just being nice to me for once."

"I'm sorry, Landy," Jason said. "I didn't think you'd take it so seriously. I thought you'd see the gold was fake and figure out there never was any real gold. I'm really, really sorry."

"Well, you'll have a lot of time to make it up to her, because you're grounded for the rest of the month," Mr. Berensen said.

Landy was numb. She stared at the ground—at her worthless heap of rock. Fool's gold. That meant gold for a fool. And who was that fool? She was—for believing that the mountains could be hiding a fortune and for falling for another one of Jason's practical jokes.

Everything around her seemed to be moving in slow motion, as in a bad dream. She noticed her parents talking to Jason and the Clarks comforting Amie. Landy quietly said good–bye to her friend and told her mother she wanted to be alone for awhile to ride with Belle.

Drained of hope and emotion and dulled by the shock, she walked over to Belle, who nuzzled her. She mounted Belle and headed for the wooded area behind the barn.

While she was angry at Jason for making her look like a fool, she was even angrier at herself. Had she really thought that just because she wanted to find gold, she would?

Landy slapped at a low hanging branch. Once again her wild imagination and big dreaming had led her to a dead end. No wonder her parents had wanted her to prove herself. Why should they give two hundred dollars to a girl who believed in legends and treasure maps?

Landy closed her eyes. And the worst thing was that she still hadn't earned enough money for the registration fee. She passed through the trees. She'd ridden happily here a million times, only today it didn't feel comforting. She felt so all alone. Landy patted and stroked Belle's neck. "If it weren't for you," she told her horse, "I would be totally lost."

Ahead of her, Landy could see the lower meadow.

She gave Belle the familiar click and loosened her rein. The pair started at an easy canter, eventually breaking into a full run. It was as if all the emotions of the past hour, day, and week leapt out with each changing step. The wind and the pace made Landy's eyes water. Suddenly, the water turned to real tears, bringing forward all the hurt Landy so desperately had tried to suppress.

As they approached the river, Belle slowed to a trot. At the river's edge, Landy let Belle drink the cold, refreshing water. Meanwhile, she slid off the saddle and slumped to the soft, musty dirt below a pine tree. Landy was not quite finished with her tears; the hurt returned. What was so wrong about wanting to go to a horse show? Why was it so silly to hope to find treasure? Why was it wrong to dream?

As the minutes passed, the hurt gradually lifted, replaced by a resolve to keep trying. Landy stood up and wiped her moist face dry. She walked over to where Belle stood and stroked her neck, looking deep into her hazel eyes. "Don't worry, girl," she said. She took a deep breath. "I haven't given up yet." Then she slipped her foot into the stirrup and swung into the saddle to ride home.

CHAPTER ELEVEN

Hidden Treasure

As Landy rode down the road to the barn, she noticed the Tremanes' white van pulling up in front of the house.

"Oh, no," she moaned. She remembered how she had bragged to Monica about finding gold. Amie had warned her to keep their find a secret, but she hadn't listened. Now she would have to pay the price. Monica had probably told everyone she had met about the gold. In the days to come she would be the town's laughingstock.

"Why didn't I listen to Amie and keep my mouth shut?" she muttered. In that instant, Landy knew how every forty-niner who'd filed a false claim had felt.

Landy tugged at Belle's reins, pulling her to a halt. She desperately wanted to turn Belle around and head back to the safety of the hills. She slumped in her seat and rested her elbows on the saddle horn. "I might as well get it over with."

As she rode closer, she saw Will and Amanda Evans as well as the Tremanes climb out of the van, and she knew she would have to face the embarrassment of telling her story from beginning to end all over again.

"Hi, Landy." Will Evans greeted her with a friendly wave. "Monica said you and Amie found something up in the mountains."

Landy swung off Belle and tied her to the small hitching post at the bottom of the front porch steps. "It was nothing, really."

Monica stepped forward. "Now, now, don't try to hide it. You were bursting about some big claim."

"Look, it was all a mistake," Landy said.

"You mean you lied?" Monica snapped.

"No, I didn't lie. It's just that we didn't really find gold."

"Would you mind showing us what you did find?" Amanda asked.

"I'd rather not. Let's just leave it that I was fooled like a lot of other prospectors."

"I'd still like to take a look," Amanda insisted.

Landy sighed. "Okay. But it's just fool's gold, common pyrite."

The group followed Landy to the spot where they had dumped their saddlebags and lowered the chest. Mr. and Mrs. Berensen heard the voices and joined the group. Landy introduced her parents to Will and Amanda.

Amanda picked up a nugget of pyrite. "These are beautiful specimens," she said. "I can see why you were fooled. They do look like gold."

"That was the point," Landy said. "My brother planted them to make us think we had found real gold."

Monica stood in front of Landy with her arms crossed, shaking her head. "And you fell for it?"

"Yes," Landy said. "I fell for it, hook, line, and sinker."

Meanwhile, Amanda and Will were examining the chest.

"Did you find the gold in the chest?" Will asked.

"No, we found the chest at another site. We just used it to carry the gold—I mean the pyrite—back," Landy answered.

"Where exactly did you find the chest?" Will asked.

Landy smiled. "Actually, I didn't find it; my horse, Belle, did. She led us to a cave where we unearthed the chest, but when we pried it open, it was empty."

"What do you think?" Amanda asked her brother.

"Well, I'll have to do some checking, but so far indications are strong."

Amanda nodded. "The markings are very clear."

"Yes, and the hinges are still in incredible condition." Will turned to face Landy. "Can you tell me any more about the location where you found the chest?"

"Is it important?"

Will smiled. "It could be."

"You mean that dirty old thing is valuable?" Monica asked.

"Possibly," Amanda answered.

"Really?" Landy said, beaming.

Mrs. Berensen put her arm around Landy and squeezed her.

Monica leaned in closer.

"That chest looks like the same kind of stuff Mr. Gries has in his antique shop."

Will looked over to Landy. "Actually, I was going to ask Landy for her permission to have Mr. Gries take a look at it."

"He might also have some reference books to

help us date the time period," Amanda added.

Will crouched to examine the base of the chest. "It might even have been used to transport gold back in the 1800s."

Landy stood there, stunned. Her feelings of disappointment and confusion were swiftly changing to hope and excitement.

"You just may have struck gold after all," Mr. Berensen said, ruffling Landy's hair.

"But it looks like a piece of junk," Monica howled.

"You know the old saying, 'One man's junk is another man's treasure,'" Amanda said.

"And Landy may have stumbled on real treasure," Will added.

"Let's all go to see Mr. Gries," Mrs. Berensen suggested.

"Good idea," said her husband. "Landy, why don't you unsaddle Belle, while I get Jason to help me load the chest into the truck."

Landy skipped over to the hitching post and led Belle to the barn. There she slipped off the bridle and hung it in the tack room. She scooped up some oats and poured them into the grain bin.

"You deserve every sweet bite," Landy said, as she uncinched the saddle and hung it on the rack. When she took off the saddle blanket, Belle's hair was still moist from their ride through the woods. Landy took a brush and curry comb and raised the hair to help it dry.

"I'm not promising anything," she said, as she brushed Belle's belly, "but we may have the money to go to the horse show after all." Landy checked Belle's legs to make sure there were no cuts or scratches from the day's adventure. "You know what, though? As much as I want that chest to be valuable, I know that when it comes down to it, you're my real treasure." She kissed Belle's nose. "You, my golden palomino, are worth your weight in real gold."

The sound of the pickup truck horn signaled Landy that the others were ready to head to Mr. Greis's shop.

Landy gave Belle a carrot from the tack room stash. "I'll tell you the news as soon as we get back from town."

"Hop in" her father called as he pushed open the passenger door. Landy slipped into the back seat.

"I called the Clarks, and they're going to drop Amie off at the antique store," her mother said. "I thought you'd want Amie to be there."

Landy smiled. "Thanks, Mom, I do."

The pickup rumbled past the trails that Landy had

only shortly before traveled by horseback. They rode by the Tremanes' resort, the library, and even the hardware and feed stores where they'd run errands.

Finally, they pulled into the driveway in front of Mr. Gries's antique shop. It was a quaint store with a reputation for having unique and authentic pieces.

Landy's heart skipped a beat as she shut the truck door. Amie and Will and Amanda Evans were already standing on the front porch, awaiting the arrival of the chest.

"Can you believe this?" Landy asked Amie.

Amie shook her head. "I can't believe that old dirty chest might be our treasure."

"Let's take it inside," Mr. Gries said from the top step.

Mr. Greis was a tall, slender man with rounded shoulders and a bit of a stoop. Landy figured this was because he was constantly bent over treasures from the past. His hair, thin and wispy, was a beautiful shade of silver white. He wore wire rimmed glasses with an antique chain around his neck. Another chain dangled from his breast shirt pocket. Landy had often wondered what it was for.

"Careful now," Mr. Gries directed. He motioned for Jason, Mr. Berensen, and Will to enter the shop carrying the chest. He ushered in the eager group and led them into an alcove close to the cash register. The shop was dimly lit, and the setting sun sent long rays of light through the curtained windows.

Landy sighed. Everything had a musty smell, shrouded in history. There were trinkets and boxes, as well as chairs and tables everywhere.

Jason and Will set the chest down on a maple table where a huge lamp hung overhead. Mr. Gries pulled a large volume from the shelf behind the cash register, and Amanda handed Will another book from the shelf.

Landy stepped closer to the table. She strained to hear the whispered conversation between Will, Amanda, and Mr. Gries. It seemed forever while the specialists flipped through books and old papers from Mr. Gries's files.

Landy watched Mr. Gries shake his head no, and then no again, and her heart sank. But Will seemed determined to prove his point, whatever that was. Gently he scraped the dirt from one side and the bottom of the chest. Using a delicate, yet sharp instrument, Mr. Gries shaved what appeared to be no more than a splinter from the side. He placed it under a microscope and then stepped back for Amanda and Will to examine.

Again they conferred in whispers. Landy wanted

to scream at the top of her lungs, just to make some kind of sound. Again more books and whispers. When would they know for sure?

Landy clenched her fists and walked over to Amie, who was biting her nails as she stood behind a wing-backed chair.

Suddenly Mr. Gries squatted down at the edge of the table, tugged at the gold chain from his breast pocket, and pulled out a small magnifying glass.

Will rubbed at the metal casing with a piece of cloth, Amanda wiped it with another larger one, and then Mr. Gries peered through his glass. After what seemed like an eternity, he turned to check the book and papers one more time.

Then he cleared his throat. "Well, young ladies," he said to Landy and Amie. "It appears you may have stumbled upon a strongbox from a stage robbery, circa 1852. Gold was frequently transported in chests like this one to San Francisco from the mining towns."

Landy and Amie hugged each other, as the room lit up with cheers and congratulations.

"Mr. Gries," Landy asked shyly. "Do you know of someone who'd be interested in buying the chest in the next few weeks?"

Mr. Gries smiled. "After it is documented, I can

think of a number of clients who'd be very interested, very interested indeed."

"And how much is the chest worth?" Landy continued.

Mr. Gries thought for awhile. "I should think somewhere in the neighborhood of a thousand dollars, give or take a hundred."

Landy and Amie threw their arms around each other and cheered.

Then Landy shook Mr. Gries's hand. "Thank you."

"Yes, thank you, Mr. Gries," Amie said.

Landy and Amie walked out the door and onto the porch. "We finally have our registration money," Amie said.

"And if the box is as valuable as Mr. Gries thinks, we'll also have enough for hotels, food, and our costumes," Landy said.

"Now that we're going to be rich, are you going to hire Monica's costumer in San Francisco?" Amie asked.

Landy shook her head. "I don't know about you, but I think I'll be just fine on my own. In fact, I have a whole new concept in mind."

The Golden Touch

The bright lights and warm, dry air bathed Landy's face as she and Belle waited for the final announcement of the All Around competition of the Sacramento Parade Show. She closed her eyes, soaking in all the excitement of the past few days.

The strongbox had been their real treasure. The girls had sold it for enough money for registration fees, costumes, and more. When Landy at last opened her eyes, she noticed her parents and brother in the stands. Her father flashed her the thumbs–up sign. The Clarks were also in the stands, and the two families had been enjoying a real vacation.

Landy chuckled, remembering. No, the horses

hadn't arrived in air-conditioned trailers, and the two families weren't staying in a fancy hotel or eating in luxury restaurants. But they'd splashed in the pool at their modest hotel and laughed and eaten so much food it seemed at times as if they would burst. Best of all, both girls had placed high enough to advance to the All Around competition.

And after all her talk of exotic costumes, Landy was pleased with her final choice. She sat tall and proud, adorned like an authentic forty-niner out of the California gold rush days. She wore mid-calf black boots, a sturdy pair of jeans complete with copper rivets, and a pair of white suspenders. She had bought a bolt of blue heavy cotton, and with her mother's help had made a double-breasted western shirt. As finishing touches, she had tied a red bandanna around her neck and plopped a wide-brimmed floppy hat on top of her head. Above her lip she had penciled a thin mustache.

Attached to Belle's saddle were the tools of a miner's trade. Landy had used rope and twine to bind on a miner's pan, small pick ax, dented pan, shovel, small scale, tin cup, and a bed roll. Under Belle's saddle was a heavy red blanket.

In many ways it was the most unglamorous look Landy could have imagined for herself, but it was true

to the adventure she and Belle had shared.

Landy and Amie exchanged glances. So much had happened. Why, it seemed like yesterday when they had come to their first parade class. Landy had learned so much about presentation and style. By the time the class had finished, all the riders in her division were prepared to carry their banners and start the horse show with a synchronized presentation for the stadium. Landy had even been awarded the position as lead rider.

"As we finish the final tabulations," the head judge bellowed over the loud speaker, "we ask that each participant fall into order and begin the final pass."

Landy watched the others turn and begin until she heard her number called. "Number 49," the voice echoed. The Clarks and Berensens cheered from the stands. Landy smiled. She sat tall and straight as she lowered her heels and gently squeezed them against Belle's belly. Belle walked into position, using long ground-covering strides. They began following the requirements of the pattern, weaving around the perimeter of the arena.

Landy was conscious of what the other horses were doing to avoid getting boxed. The judge called for an animated walk. A tap of the toe of Landy's boot sent Belle into an alert, relaxed pace. Landy noticed Belle's ears were pricked, a great asset. She was also quiet, had excellent control, and a responsive attitude.

Then came the call for the parade gait. As Belle pranced down the stretch, well under the required seven seconds, Landy knew with certainty that she and Belle had done their best.

Even during the earlier judging, Belle had backed immediately four steps in succession on diagonal legs in a straight line. It was sometimes her most difficult move, but not this time. Everything had gone so well, and now it was time for the field to wait for the final results.

The riders lined up in the center of the ring, side by side. Still poised, Landy let her eyes move down the line. She saw Monica tugging at her costume and struggling with a lavish Marie Antoinette white powdered wig headdress. She'd really gone too far this time, Landy thought. Her expensive tastes and costumer had created something beautiful to look at, but difficult to ride in. Landy didn't think Monica was having much fun.

Amie, on the other hand, looked elegant in her blue satin medieval costume complete with cone hat and long flowing scarf. Amie had been nervous about riding in the competition, yet had done extremely well.

The loudspeaker interrupted Landy's thoughts. "We have the results," the judge boomed. As the judge read the first name from his list of names, Landy felt her heart leap.

The riders who had placed sixth, fifth, and fourth rode out and received their awards. There were only three more names to call. Would hers and Belle's be among them? Landy tightened her reins slightly so Belle wouldn't get skittish and patted her neck for reassurance.

"Third place goes to Amie Clark and her mare, Copper."

Landy whooped with excitement, whistling and clapping her leather-gloved hands along with the audience.

Amie's face was bright red as she rode out to receive her flowers, ribbon, and trophy. Landy gave her the thumbs–up sign as she rode her victory lap.

"Second place is awarded to Jeff Kelly." Landy applauded and remembered how well this pair had worked together. She bit her bottom lip and tried to convince her stomach to settle down.

The time had come for the final announcement. Landy was happy to be at the show, but she knew deep down inside she'd ridden well, and she wanted to place.

"The ten-to-fourteen-year-old All Around Parade champion is Landy Berensen and her palomino mare, Queen Isabella del Conquistador."

As she rode out to receive her bouquet, ribbon, and gold trophy, Landy could see her parents hugging each other in the stands. Even Jason was on his feet cheering. All her past struggles and triumphs melded into this one thrilling moment.

"Let's give another hand to our gold digger from Caribou, California," the announcer boomed.

Holding her trophy high above her head in the stadium lights, Landy threw back her head and soaked in the crowd's deafening applause.

FACTS
ABOUT THE BREED

You probably know a lot about palominos from reading this book. Here are some more interesting facts about this golden horse.

Ω Although palomino is a color type and not a breed, a number of organizations register palomino horses. The active palomino registries include the Golden American Saddlebred Horse Association, which registers palomino Saddlebreds; the Palomino Horse Association; Palomino Horse Breeders of America; and Palomino Ponies of America.

Ω Color is the palomino's most prominent feature. Unfortunately, the lovely golden color of the palomino coat cannot be bred with certainty. Even if a horse breeder crosses two palominos, there is only a fifty-percent chance that the offspring will also be palomino.

∩ To be a true palomino the horse's coat color must fall within three shades of the color of a newly minted gold coin. The mane and tail must be white with less than fifteen percent dark hairs.

∩ The characteristics of a palomino depend on the horse's parentage. Palominos are often the product of a palomino and a chestnut Arabian, Thoroughbred, or Quarter Horse. The palomino–chestnut cross is thought to produce the best coloring in the offspring.

∩ The palomino coat color appears in neither pure Thoroughbreds nor pure Arabians. There are, however, purebred Quarter Horses and Saddlebred with palomino coats. Recently, there has been an increase in the number of palomino Morgans.

⌒ No one is sure where these golden horses got their name. Some people think that they were named after a Spanish grape with a similar golden color. Others think they got their name from Juan de Palomino, a Spanish nobleman. Still others think the name comes from the Spanish word for *dove–paloma.*

⌒ In Spain horses with palomino coloring sometimes are called Isabella. This name is thought to honor Queen Isabella (1451–1501), who loved the palomino coloring and promoted it.

⌒ There were palominos among the first horses brought to the New World by Spanish explorers. These golden–coated horses even appear in Chinese art dating from 220 B.C.

∩ A few palominos have become famous. Mr. Ed, whose original name was Bamboo Harvester, played a talking horse on his own television show from 1961 to 1966. Before this starring role, he formed part of the Palomino Parade in the Tournament of Roses.

∩ Roy Rogers, the "King of the Cowboys," rode a palomino stallion named Trigger. Roy and Trigger starred in their own television show from 1952 to 1957. If you visit the Roy Rogers Museum in Victorville, California, you can see Trigger. He is displayed mounted and rearing, the way so many people remember him.

∩ In Scotland people tell stories about a palomino horse. According to legend, one foggy day the Golden Horse of Loch Lundy appeared to two fishermen who had just brought their boat ashore. One of the men was determined to catch the glistening horse despite his friend's pleas for caution. He jumped onto the horse's back. The horse reared up with a shrill whinny and charged into the hills. The man was never seen again.

∩ Despite this ominous legend, palominos are popular all over the world. While the United States is home to the most extensive palomino breeding, there is also a Danish Palomino Breeders Association.

∩ In the United States palominos are particularly popular out west. There they are used as parade horses and as stock horses. Stock horses are used for working with livestock—herding, roping, and cutting.

∩ In horse shows palominos also appear in hunter and jumper classes and in pleasure classes under both Western and English tack. The golden palomino is as versatile as it is colorful.